To:

From:

Why a Son Needs a Mom

by Gregory E. Lang   pictures by Gail Yerrill

Adapted for picture book by Susanna Leonard Hill

sourcebooks
wonderland

From the moment that I saw your beautiful face,

held you close to my heart in a mother's embrace,

I promised to help you grow with strength and grace.

My dear one, my sweet son, my boy.

Crayon self-portraits and daisy bouquets,

crooked *I love you*s at each Mother's Day,

I'll cherish your sweetness and presents always.

The gift I most treasure is you.

Good-natured, spirited, fearless, and true,

clever, affectionate, purposeful too,

if the world gets you down, fails to see the real you,

please have faith in yourself as I do.

Together we'll race, fight with pillows, climb trees,

jump rope, and swing high like a pair of monkeys,

but also we'll snuggle together, at ease,

strong body, calm mind, busy boy.

I'll teach you to listen to what makes you hum,

march to the beat of your own unique drum.

Only YOU know the person you want to become.

Be your own perfect self and stand proud.

Sometimes your mischief may get out of hand.

And though things can turn out not exactly as planned,

just be honest and know that I will understand.

I'll guide you the next time around.

I'll wonder with you at the world's little things.

Silvery spider webs, honeycomb rings,

shooting stars, rainbows, and hummingbird wings.

Notice beauty and stay curious too.

I know that making mistakes can be tough.

Finding courage to say you were wrong's really rough.

But hold your head high. You are *always* enough.

I'll be right there beside you, brave boy.

Take time for dreaming a little each day.

Imagine, be silly, and let your thoughts play!

Wish on a star with your mind far away.

Anything is possible! It's true.

I'll be there if you fall, bump your nose, scrape your knee,

have a really bad day, or get stung by a bee.

It's okay to cry! You can always find me

to comfort and listen with love.

Stand up for what you believe to be right,

but know that not everything is worth a fight.

Sometimes just talking achieves more than might.

Choose understanding, kindness, and care.

Sometimes despite when you give it your all,

things don't work out, and it makes you feel small.

I'll help you remember to keep standing tall.

Don't give up, my unstoppable boy.

Be gentle with those who are different from you.

Make an effort to understand new points of view.

And don't be afraid to try something new.

Our differences make us unique.

Keep your heart open to all that's to come.

There are so many marvelous things to be done!

Change in the world begins with you, son.

I know you'll use your voice for good.

From the boy that you are to the man you will be,

I love who you are and the promise I see.

You make me the mother I dreamed I could be.

My dear one, my sweet son, my joy.

To Mom, with love and devotion. —GEL

With love for my little bunny—not so little anymore! —SLH

For my mum and mum- and dad-in-law, you're all amazing!
And to my Abigail and William—Love you always xox —GY

Published by Sourcebooks Wonderland, an imprint of Sourcebooks Kids
P.O. Box 4410, Naperville, Illinois 60567–4410
(630) 961-3900
sourcebookskids.com

Library of Congress Cataloging-in-Publication Data is on file with the publisher.

Source of Production: 1010 Printing Asia Limited, Kwun Tong, Hong Kong, China
Date of Production: March 2022
Run Number: 5025517
Printed and bound in China.
OGP 10 9 8 7 6